Celebrating
Birthdays

By: Shelly Nielsen
Illustrated by: Marie-Claude Monchaux

T 31663

LIBRARY
PARKSIDE ELEMENTARY SCHOOL
BUFFALO, MINNESOTA 55313

Published by Abdo & Daughters, 4940 Viking Drive, Suite 622, Edina, Minnesota 55435.

Library bound edition distributed by Rockbottom Books, Pentagon Tower, P.O. Box 36036, Minneapolis, Minnesota 55435.

Copyright © 1996 by Abdo Consulting Group, Inc., Pentagon Tower, P.O. Box 36036, Minneapolis, Minnesota 55435 USA. International copyrights reserved in all countries. No part of this book may be reproduced in any form without written permission from the publisher.

Printed in the United States.

Illustrations by Marie-Claude Monchaux.

Edited by Julie Berg

Library of Congress Cataloging-in-Publication Data

Nielsen, Shelly, 1958-
    Birthdays / Shelly Nielsen.
        p. cm. -- (Holiday Celebrations)
    Summary: Rhyming text introduces aspects of this important day.
    ISBN 1-56239-706-0
       1. Birthdays--Juvenile literature.[1.Birthdays.]I. Title.
II. Series: Nielsen, Shelly, 1958-Holiday celebrations.
GT2430.N54 1996
394.2--dc20
                                                96-12761
                                                    CIP
                                                      AC

Celebrating
Birthdays

Endless Wait

The weeks before my birthday
seem to creep along.
They move as slow as cold molasses,
my birthday never comes.
Then suddenly, the days speed up.
The waiting's almost done.
Start the countdown—
Here we go:
Five ...
    Four ...
        Three ...
            Two ...
                One ...

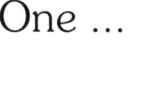

Another Year...

Do I look taller?
Brighter?
Bolder?
That's funny;
I thought I might.
I feel different from head to toe
because today I'm a whole year older.

Card & Greetings

Mail's here! I'll get it!
What do I see?
Envelopes with my name on them.
Three birthday cards for me!

There's one from Grandma,
one from my friend, Ann,
and one from Uncle Ted.
Three birthday cards in one afternoon;
how lucky can you get?

Cake Dreams

I'm dreaming of a birthday cake
with layers miles high.
Chocolate frosting
two feet thick,
and candles that reach the sky.
This cake has a million sprinkles
and luscious chocolate curls.
If I ever got a cake like that
I'd be one happy girl!

Queen for a Day

In this crown my teacher made
I'm birthday queen for a day.
Do I look taller?
Brighter?
Bolder?
A queen feels grand
when she's a whole year older!

A Birthday Song

Surprise!
Between spelling and math
my teacher led
the "happy birthday" song
with the whole class singing along.
Of course I liked it,
but I squirmed.
My face turned red and burned.
Next month,
I can relax.
It'll be someone else's turn!

Special Lunch

Sandwich ... celery ... carrots ...
What's this?
A lunchbox note to me
smashed beneath
an apple
and a chocolate chip cookie.
"Happy birthday from Mom and Dad
to our dearest one.
Hurry home right after school
for kisses, hugs, and fun."

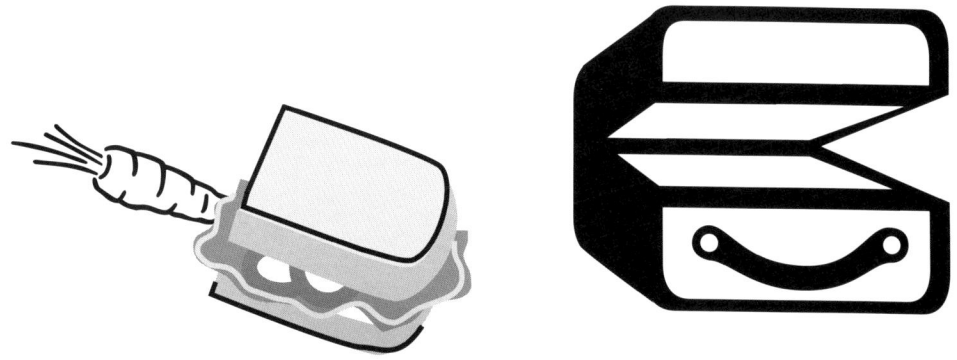

Big Balloons

Shiny balloons—
red, green, yellow.
Perfect for your party,
you lucky birthday fellow.

So what are you waiting for?
Let's blow them up.
Puff - puff! Too full! Stop!
Too late!
Pop!

Pin the Tail...

'Round and 'round I spin,
a blindfold over my eyes.
If I pin the donkey tail just right
I could win a prize.
There! I did it! Can I look?
I hear my laughing friends.
The donkey's tail is firmly pinned
where the nose should have been!

A Birthday Tune for My Friend

"Happy birthday to you,"
I sing out of tune.
You pretend not to like it
but your smile says you do.

So "Happy birthday to you,"
from a friend who's true blue.
You can get me back next month
when you sing to me, too.

Telephone--For Me?

"Hello, Grandson.
Though I'm far away,
I wish I could see how you've grown;
so I'm sending good wishes
and birthday kisses
and hugs by telephone."

Thank You, Thank You

I loved your gift!
Just wanted to let you know.
To prove it, I've signed this note,
with two X's and an O.